RYAN
AND THE
CIRCUS
WHEELS

Chariot Books is an imprint of David C. Cook Publishing Co.
David C. Cook Publishing Co., Elgin, Illinois 60120
David C. Cook Publishing Co., Weston, Ontario

RYAN AND THE CIRCUS WHEELS

Cover design by Dawn Lauck

First printing, 1988
Printed in U.S.A.
92 91 90 89 88   1 2 3 4 5

Library of Congress Cataloging-in-Publication Data

Tada, Joni Eareckson, 1949—
  Ryan and the circus wheels/by Joni Eareckson Tada; illustrated by Norman McGary.

  Summary: Ryan is ashamed of his sister when she fills in as room mother and takes his class to the
circus, because she is in a wheelchair; but then when he gets separated from the group God uses her
wheels to help him get back on the right track.
  [1. Physically handicapped—Fiction. 2. Circus—Fiction. 3. Christian life—Fiction.] I. McGary, Norman,
ill. II Title.
PZ7.T116Ry   1988   87-26912
ISBN 1-555-13154-9

circus! A real circus with tents and everything," squealed Jennifer from the front seat of the van.

"Yeah," said Josh in the backseat. "And there'll be tigers and lions . . . rowrrl!" He growled and sank his fingers like claws into Jennifer's shoulders.

Ryan sat slumped in the back, his eyes down and his arms folded across his chest.

Ordinarily, the idea of a three-ring circus with lions and tigers would make him tingle, too. But this class trip wasn't turning out the way Ryan thought it would be: his sister Shannon, of all people, was filling in as room mother. Now all his friends knew the truth . . . his sister was in a wheelchair.

"Quiet down now, kids," Shannon said as she steered the van into the parking lot, but neither Jennifer nor Josh nor any of the other kids paid any attention.

That's because she's in a wheelchair, thought Ryan. He gathered his things and piled out of the van with the rest. *Who cares what people in wheelchairs say?*

Shannon tried to keep the group in line. They could hear lions roaring, food vendors shouting, and a pipe organ blasting out a dancing tune. A circle of juggling clowns practiced their balancing act while a huge elephant and her baby stood sleepily nearby.

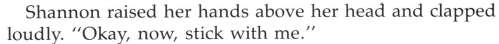

Shannon raised her hands above her head and clapped loudly. "Okay, now, stick with me."

Ryan stayed at the back of the group. In her wheelchair, he noticed, his sister was shorter than all of his friends. *I wonder what they think about a "room mother" who's shorter than they are.*

With Ryan still lagging behind, the group's first stop was at a red popcorn wagon, puffing and steaming and popping fresh corn. Shannon counted everyone's raised hand and placed her order with the jolly man in a red-striped apron.

"Thanks, Shannon," said the kids as they scooped up handfuls of hot, salty popcorn. Jennifer flung her arms around Shannon's neck. "Can I push you next?" she asked.

"I can tell you're a great pusher," Shannon answered, "but my brother hasn't had a turn yet. Ryan, would you like to help?"

Everyone looked at Ryan, but he just shrugged and nibbled some popcorn. When he didn't respond, Jennifer took her place behind Shannon's chair while the others jumped and skipped about.

Ryan watched his sister lead the way. She pointed directions and everyone followed. *They're just following to be nice to her, he reasoned.* Then he felt crummy for thinking such a thought.

Shannon took her place in the ticket line like everyone else. An organ grinder's monkey climbed up the spokes of her wheels, and all the kids laughed.

Shannon watched and waved as the group rode the merry-go-round. She parked outside the bathroom and waited for Ryan and his friends.

I bet everyone feels sorry for her, Ryan thought.

Ryan walked slower and slower. He was so busy thinking about Shannon and her wheelchair, he stopped paying attention to where the group was heading. The next thing he knew, he looked up and they were gone!

"Josh! Jennifer!" he shouted above the noise of pipe organs and peanut vendors. No one answered.

"Shannon!" he called, dropping his popcorn and pushing his way through the crowd. "Shannon, where are you?"

Ryan tripped and fell against somebody in a green polka-dot suit with a large tummy that seemed far too soft. He looked up into the face of a clown.

"Do you know where my sister is?"

"Why, no, little boy," said the clown, as he shifted and straightened the pillows around his middle. "But don't be afraid. I'll help you find her."

Ryan said a quick prayer inside his head. And no sooner had he asked God for help, than an idea dawned. "I know how to find her!" he declared. "I'll just follow the tracks!"

"But how—" started the clown, but Ryan had already darted off.

The sawdust was good for tracking—only there were so *many* tracks. Tennis shoes. High heels. Boots. Even horseshoes. Suddenly he saw them—wheel tracks. He was on the right trail. Ryan rounded the corner of a tent.

"Rowrrrrl!" A powerful tiger snarled at Ryan from his cage.

"Oh, my!" Ryan exclaimed to the tiger trainer. "I thought he was my sister!"

"Your sister?!" the trainer laughed. "I don't think so. At least, you don't look like a tiger to me! Can I help you find her?"

Ryan knelt by the brightly colored wheels of the cage. They were wide with wooden edges. How could he have mistaken their tracks for Shannon's? Suddenly he spotted another set of tracks. He was on the trail again.

Ryan followed Shannon's tracks through the sawdust, around three bales of hay, and in and out of a mud puddle. He almost got confused by the tracks of an ice-cream cart. A moment later, the wooden wheels of a cotton candy wagon crossed his path.

Ryan felt a moment of panic. People jostled and pushed in every direction. *Please, God,* prayed Ryan, *don't let me get off the right trail!* Then he spotted a wheelbarrow filled with feed. Ryan waved as he ran by two clowns on bicycles. There were wheels everywhere—but he knew which tracks belonged to Shannon.

Ryan was sure he was hot on the trail. Then, suddenly, something was wrong. One track crossed over the other. Sometimes the wheel tracks were close together; other times they were very far apart. Just then, one of the tracks made a big circle while the other continued straight. Shannon's chair couldn't do that! Then Ryan saw who was making the tracks.

Two acrobats on unicycles!

Ryan felt like crying, but he stopped and prayed once more. Then he examined the ground. Those *had* to be Shannon's tracks—and they led him straight ahead.

Ryan rounded a stack of straw.

There were Shannon and his classmates waiting by the entrance to the circus tent.

"There he is!" shouted Jennifer, and the other kids cheered. "You found us!"

Ryan ran right past them into the open arms of his sister. He nearly tipped her chair up on one wheel, he gave her such a big hug.

"Oh, Shannon," Ryan blurted out, "I'll never be—" He felt his cheeks get red. Then he took a deep breath, looked her straight in the eyes, and continued. "I'll never be embarrassed about your wheelchair again. God used your wheels to lead me right to you!"

"Hey, neat!" Josh said. "Let us get lost, Shannon, and then try to find you by your wheels!"

The other kids clapped their hands. "Please, Shannon?"

Ryan turned and smiled at his classmates. They really did like his sister. In fact, they even seemed to like her wheelchair! They thought she was different, but in a special way, not a mean one.

Ryan felt ashamed. *He* was the one with the not-so-nice thoughts. As he watched, Josh and Jennifer moved to either side of Shannon to give her a hug. Suddenly Ryan noticed something else. Sure, Shannon was short in her wheelchair—but that just made her easier to hug!

*A*ll of us have bad thoughts once in a while. The problem gets worse when, like Ryan, we let our bad thoughts go on and on. They might be angry thoughts about God or unkind thoughts about other people. Before we know it, those thoughts fill our minds and we lose track of what we really want to be doing or thinking.

Like Ryan, we need to get our thoughts back in line by praying. We need to get back on the "right track." God's Word says, "Whatever is right, whatever is pure, whatever is lovely, whatever is admirable—if anything is excellent or praiseworthy—think about such things" (Philippians 4:8, NIV).

When Ryan discovered that, it made all the difference in the way he thought about Shannon and her wheelchair. It can work for you, too. The next time you're thinking thoughts that are mean or hurtful, ask God to help you to get back on track! He's always listening, and He's always ready to help.